SIGN OF THE DRAGON

C.M. Eddy, Jr.

(Frontispiece by John Betancourt)

SIGN OF THE DRAGON

C.M. EDDY, JR.

WILDSIDE PRESS

INTRODUCTION

Clifford Martin Eddy Jr. (1896–1967), who published as C. M. Eddy Jr., was an American author known for his horror, mystery, and supernatural short stories. He is best remembered for his work in *Weird Tales* magazine and his friendship with H. P. Lovecraft.

Eddy was born in Providence, Rhode Island. He went to Classical High School in Providence, and as a child was a precocious reader and writer. He continued to be an avid reader and writer, interested in mythology and the occult, for his entire life. According to his wife Muriel:

> Cliff was always interested in the idea of parallel planes—where life on another level, either astral or otherwise, would be similar to that on earth—or where life might exist, but in another time or another form. He was also fascinated by the themes of teleportation, vampirism, ghosts, and the mystery of unexplained phenomena...he spent hours in the library researching the unusual, the unique, the bizarre.

He began his career writing with a short novel, *Sign of the Dragon* (*Mystery Magazine*, 1919), a detective story, but soon branched out to writing for a broad range of pulp fiction magazines, including *Weird Tales*, *Munsey's Magazine*, and *Snappy Stories*. His tales of mystery, ghosts, and song-writing (he also wrote songs, including "When We Met by the Blue Lagoon," "In My Wonderful Temple of Love," "Dearest of All," "Underneath the Whispering Pine," "Sunset Hour," and others.) His fiction began to include elements of songs and song-writing.

The Eddys' first contact with H. P. Lovecraft occurred as early as 1918. They first met face-to-face in August 1923, according to Muriel Eddy—they were introduced by Eddy's and Lovecraft's mothers, both of whom were active in the women's suffrage movement.

After that, Lovecraft frequently visited the Eddys' home on Second Street in East Providence, and later called on them at their home in the Fox Point section of Providence. Eddy rapidly became a member of Lovecraft's inner circle of friends and authors, and he and Lovecraft edited each other's works. Both he and Lovecraft were also ghost-writers for Harry Houdini, collaborating on "The Cancer of Superstition," for the magician, but Houdini's death in 1926 curtailed the project. (Notes and surviving fragments of the collaboration were later published in *The Dark Brotherhood and Other Pieces*.)

Eddy and Lovecraft took scenic walks, including one to the Old Stone Mill in Newport, Rhode Island; August Derleth later incorporated notes taken by Lovecraft on this occasion into The Lurker at the Threshold.

Muriel Eddy typed many of Lovecraft's manuscripts, and Lovecraft would often read his stories to the couple. Eddy wrote several stories that were published in *Weird Tales* during 1924 and 1925: "The Ghost Eater" (a werewolf tale), 1924; "The Loved Dead" (about demoniac desire for the dead), 1924; and "Deaf, Dumb and Blind" (a chronicle of Satanic sensations), 1925. Lovecraft's contribution seems to have ranged from making suggestions and perhaps a paragraph change. These early C.M. Eddy stories were later collected in *The Loved Dead and Other Tales*.

Other stories by Eddy which appeared in *Weird Tales* during 1924 and 1925 were "Ashes" (about an experiment by a chemistry professor), 1924; "With Weapons of Stone" (a story of prehistoric man), 1924; "Arhl-a of the Caves" (another prehistory tale); and "The Better Choice" (about a machine for reviving the dead), 1925.

In August 1923, Eddy and Lovecraft sought the Dark Swamp, a place of which Lovecraft had heard rumours and which was said to lie "off the Putnam Pike, about halfway between Chepachet, Rhode Island and Putnam, Connecticut." The legend surrounding the place (which they never found) seems to have influenced the opening of Lovecraft's story "The Colour Out of Space" (1927).

The Dark Swamp was also the basis for Eddy's unfinished short story "Black Noon" (1967) (posthumously published in *Exit into Eternity: Tales of the Bizarre and Supernatural*, see below). The introduction to *Exit Into Eternity* explains that Eddy was unable to complete the work due to illness, and died in 1967; also that August Derleth was intending to finish this work, and perhaps expand it into a full-length novel, but it remained unfinished due to Derleth's death in 1971. The protagonist of "Black Noon" is a pipe-smoking businessman called Biff Briggs (standing in for Eddy himself— "Biff" instead of "Cliff") who reads pulp magazines in his spare time. After discovering the work of a superb horror writer named Robert Otis Mather (a thinly veiled fictitious version of H. P. Lovecraft) in the new pulp *Uncanny Stories* and finding he lives in the same town, Briggs befriends him and becomes a frequent visitor to Mathers' house at 31 Spring Lane, Fenham. (This fictitious town was invented by Eddy and is featured in "The Loved Dead" and "Deaf, Dumb and Blind" (1924). Mathers (known as Rom for short, due to his initials), is partly cared for by his aunt, Agatha Sessions. Mathers writes a trilogy of novels which seem to have taken him over almost by demonic possession. In the summer, Rom wants to investigate a town called Granville, which is reputed to have numerous haunted houses, and calls on Briggs to transport him. Over a period of two weeks they hold nightly vigils awaiting supernatural manifestations; while no ghosts appear, Rom's life is nearly ended several times by seemingly unnatural accidents.

C.M. Eddy was also a theatrical booking agent for 25 years, promoting shows that featured many famous vaudevillians and performers of the early twentieth century. In later years, he was a proofreader for Oxford Press, a principal clerk at the business management office of the Rhode Island State Department of Public Health, secretary treasurer of the Rhode Island Theatrical Booking Agents' Association, and president (1954–1956) and treasurer (1962–67) of the Rhode Island Writers' Guild. He died on November 21, 1967, aged 71, and is interred at Swan Point Cemetery.

—Karl Wurf
Rockville, Maryland

CHAPTER ONE

AN OATH OF ALLEGIANCE

WHEN MY FATHER WAS stricken one morning in April, Death was the farthest from my thoughts. I looked upon it, as did Mrs. Waynemore, the housekeeper, as a passing illness. But, as he grew steadily worse, Doctor Barnes, who had known me since he helped usher me into this old world, said to me to hope for the best, but to be prepared for the worst. At last came the day when the doctor told the old gentleman that his hours were numbered, that he had done all in his power to stay the onward march of the Grim Reaper. Father listened to the verdict of the physician, and asked that I be summoned. My heart was heavy as I went in and took my place at his bedside.

He was quite calm, but I could detect a suppressed excitement in his eyes as he asked the doctor and the housekeeper to retire. In spite of its sadness my heart beat a little faster as they left the room, and I began to wonder what it could be that he wanted of me—alone. As soon as he was sure that the others were safely out of hearing, he indicated a seat for me by the head of the bed.

"Chester," he began, before I leave this old world I want to tell you a tale out of my life that I have never told you before. I want you to listen without interruption, for my time is short and I want to be sure that it is finished before I pass on."

He paused for a moment, as if doubtful just how to begin.

"I was just a bit older than you are now, and I had seen pretty much of the world, even at that age. But no matter where I roamed, I always came back to Manorport sooner or later. It was the only real home I knew. I had been back from my last trip just a few days. My pockets were well lined, for my last venture had been a profitable one. We all have our hobbies and mine has always been the acquisition of curios in the way of jewelry or trinkets, worthless except for their oddity. I was somehow reminded of a peculiar ring I had marked in a little Chinese shop, on the waterfront in Boston, which I had passed on my way home a few days before. I was possessed of an uncontrollable desire to add it to my collection. The desire for that ring grew upon me all throughout the day, and I spent a sleepless night because of it. The next morning I left Manorport intent only upon acquiring it. The shop I mentioned was in rather an unsavory section of the city, but I knew my Boston well. Many was the oddity I had picked up in this selfsame shop. The Chinaman who ran the place—Len Sang he called himself—knew me for a regular customer. My luck must have been sidetracked somehow. When I reached the shop I found, to my dismay, that the ring was gone from the window. There was no need of 'pidgin' English with Len Sang. I don't know where he learned, but he could speak our language as well as I.

"'Yes,' he told me, 'I remember well the ring you have in mind. Was it not a silver ring, with a peculiar setting? A Chinese dragon, with eyes of jade?'

"'That's the one I came all the way back here to get,' I told him. 'Where is it? I want to buy it.'

"'It is gone, sir. I sold it only last evening.'

"'Sold it! But I must have it!' The desire for that ring was becoming an obsession.

"'But yes,' he returned; 'wait but a moment.'

"He disappeared into the back room of the shop. When he returned, he had in his hand what I could have sworn was the self-same ring I had seen in the shop window.

"'Sly dog! I thought you told me you had sold it,' I accused him.

"'Aye, sir, and so I did.' He bowed. 'This is its mate. There were only two of these rings ever made. The one I sold last evening to the customer I mentioned. This ring is its exact duplicate.'

"That rather savored of mystery, and I asked him if by chance the rings had a history.

"'All that I know,' he responded, 'is that a few weeks ago a little old man came into the store with these two rings to sell me. He told me they had been made especially for two Chinese nobleman, whose names and peculiarities I well knew, and were worn by them until their recent death. He claimed that they were the only rings of their kind ever made. How he came into possession of them, or his right to sell them, I did not question. We seldom question such rights here. I was taken by the peculiar character of the rings, so I bought them, almost at my own price. One I put in the window, where it has remained until last night; the other is here.'

"He passed it over the counter for my inspection.

"I was rather skeptical about the story he told of the rings and how they came into his possession. It came too readily to his lips to carry any weight with me. From what I knew of Len Sang, he was, like most of the others of his race, secretive and taciturn. To find him loquacious was to make me suspicious that he must have a reason, for being so.

"I did not give him any inkling of my doubts, however, but began haggling with him over the price of the remaining ring. Len Sang was a shrewd business man, and he knew I wanted the ring badly. Finally we came to terms, I forgot just what the ring cost me, but Len Sang was no loser, of that I am certain.

"Len Sang bowed me all the way to the door of the shop, a sleepy, oily, shop-worn smile on his saffron face, thanking me profusely all the while for my custom. I was sorry, of course, that I had not been able to acquire the pair of rings, but I rather congratulated myself on my luck in their being a second one that I might buy. My bargaining had made me rather thirsty, so I made for a nearby grog-shop to quench my thirst and provide myself with an opportunity to examine my purchase more closely.

"I had settled myself with my half-and-half when I spied some one whom I had not seen in an age. It was 'Spike' Burgess; a big hulking brute of a man, but as good-hearted a chap as had ever been my good fortune to meet. Many a wild time we had weathered together and escaped unscathed. He was the only real 'pal' I had ever had, and I'd been lonesome enough. drifting around since I saw him last, two years before. I hailed him, and he came lumbering over to my table.

"'Peter Brent, by all that's holy! Where have you been keeping yourself? Damn it all, old man, I'm glad to see you!'

"His mighty fist came down upon the table in emphasis of his remark with a crash that nearly splintered the boards of the table itself. I gripped the brawny hand he extended, and we settled down to talk over the things that had happened since we had last seen one another.

"We exchanged confidences freely, for at that hour of the day the saloon was well-nigh deserted. At length I bethought myself of my latest purchase. I slipped it off my finger and held it up for Spike's inspection.

"I was totally unprepared for the effect it had upon him. At the sight of it his eyes dilated, his hands gripped the edges of the table so tightly that the muscles on his arms stood out like whipcords, and the perspiration ran down his face in streams.

"'Good God, man!' he rasped, his voice hoarse and unnatural, 'where did you get that ring?'

"'Why the excitement, Spike?' I questioned. 'I bought that ring at Len Sang's, not more than a couple hours ago.'

"The terror slowly faded from his eyes.

"'It's all right, Peter, as long as you bought it,' he returned; 'but the last time I saw that ring, or its mate, was in Hong Kong. It was there I heard the legend that goes with it. If you'll satisfy me by putting that ring back in you pocket before some one else sees it, we'll take a little walk and I'll tell you in a few words why I was so upset at the sight of it.'

"Back went the ring into my pocket, and we strolled aimlessly along the waterfront while he told me the tale he heard about the dragon rings.

"'The rings are nearly as old as the legend itself, Peter,' he went on. 'No one knows who made them, or for whom they were made. But they are supposed to possess this peculiar property. To anyone into whose possession they come legitimately, that person will have good luck and protection against all evil. But, should one of them be stolen, the charm is broken. Instead sudden death is in store for the culprit, and grave danger for the owner of the other until the stolen ring has been recovered, or until the thief disposes of it in some way. The last time I saw one of those rings, it was on the finger of a dead Chinese shop-keeper, in Hong Kong. No one knew how he had come to his death, but it was rumored that the ring had come into his possession by questionable means.'

"'But why the concern, Spike, at my simply having one of the rings in my possession? You didn't think I had stolen it, did you?'

"'No, but someone else might. The news is all over the waterfront that Len Stang's was entered last night, and the mate to that ring stolen from the show-window. It's a wonder you hadn't heard. I'd advise you to keep it out of sight until you get safely away from here.'

"Then I knew the reason for Len Sang's talkative mood of the morning. He knew the legend of the rings, without a doubt; but he was afraid, should I learn it, he would be unable to dispose of the remaining ring, with its attendant danger for the owner.

"'I've been up home in Manorport the last few days, so I haven't heard any of the news down around here,' I explained. 'I saw the ring in the show-window when I passed the shop on the way home. I came down to Boston today on purpose to buy it.' Then I told him of Len Stang's story of how he acquired the rings, and the sale of the other the night before.

"'Smooth-tongued devil!' Spike commented.

"Then, as if dismissing the subject, 'Where are you headed, matey?'

"'I'm going back up to Manorport and rest up for a little while. After that, the Lord only knows. Say Spike,' with a sudden inspiration, 'come along up home and spend the night with me. I'm all alone, you know.

"He thought it over for a while, and not being able to think up any excuse that I would stand for, accepted the invitation.

"Trains weren't as frequent in those days as they are now, Chester, and it was well along towards ten o'clock before we reached Manorport.

"As we made our way along the deserted main street, Spike caught my arm and drew me into the shadow of one of the buildings.

"'I've a feeling we're being followed,' he told me.

"I laughed at him. 'What's the matter with you, anyhow, today, Spike? You're as nervous as an old woman. Just a while ago I thought your eyes would pop out of your head at the mere sight of a ring, and now —'

"He swung me out of harm's way just in time. I could feel the swish as the keen blade of a knife fanned my cheek, slashing through the air at the exact spot I had been but a moment before.

"In a flash, Spike was on my assailant. Silently they locked together in a struggle for the possession of that keen, gleaming, ugly blade.

"Back and forth they struggled, neither uttering a sound. I was helpless to take any active part in the fray, lest I dislodge Spike's grip upon the man's wrist. If that happened, one of us was as good as dead.

"At last Spike's tremendous weight began to tell. Inch by inch he forced my assailant back over his knee, till they were bent double. Suddenly the knife flashed free, as Spike aimed it at the body of the man who attacked us. He sank to the pavement without a sound.

"We rolled the man over to see who was responsible for our adventure, and looked down into the yellow face of the Chinaman who used to work around Len Sang's.

"And there, on the finger of the hand that had sought to take my life, gleamed the mate to the ring that reposed in my pocket. The legend of the ring had once more worked itself out completely.

"I took from his finger the ring which had been the cause of the trouble. We reached my home at last, and safe in the rooms I occupied, we examined the rings closely. They were just as much alike as two peas in a pod. Far into the night we sat up talking over old times, but always our conversation would revert to the subject of the rings on the table before us. They seemed to hold a strange fascination, somehow. The jade eyes gleamed up at us with a hint of mystery, and power, that enthralled us. At last I was imbued with a big idea.

"'Spike,' I announced, 'you have saved my life tonight. Many's the close shave you and I have had together; many's the time when our necks have been in danger; but tonight, had it not been for you, it would be I who lies dead out there upon the street instead of that Chinaman. I owe you a debt of gratitude. Take one of these rings. If ever you—or should you settle down some day, any of your family after you—need any assistance of any kind, even at the risk of life itself, the sign of the dragon, the symbol of this ring, will bring that assistance from me or mine.'

"He protested at first, but finally, over the table, in the early morning hours, we took a solemn oath of allegiance before God, to be handed down, if necessary, to the next generation, that Brent or Burgess, whichever the case might be, would respond to the 'Sign of the Dragon' and render assistance to the limit of his ability and power.

"The next morning he left me, and from that day to this I have never seen him. I heard, a few years later, that he had married and settled down, just as I had done, but in all those years I have had no ward from him. That night, over the table, with the dragon eyes of the ring gleaming oddly in the lamplight, is just as vivid in my memory as if it had happened yesterday. I want your promise Chester, that, should occasion ever arise, you will keep the oath I swore that night, and lend all assistance in your power, even at the risk of your life."

As he finished his story, father reached beneath his pillow and passed me the most peculiar ring I had ever seen. It was a heavy silver land, with a wonderfully wrought dragon embossed upon it, and worked in green gold. Its eyes were of jade.

"This is the ring, Chester. Somewhere is the mate to it, an exact duplicate, the only other one like it in existence. You have heard my story. Can I depend upon you to take up the promise and live it out to the letter? It is my last wish, Chester."

I felt enthralled with the weirdness of it all. It was the adventure I had longed for, prayed for, all my life. How could I do otherwise than assent to his wishes?

"Dad," I told him, "as God is my judge, I swear to respond to the sign of this dragon ring if it should ever call to me."

"Chester," he returned, "the word of a Brent is good as gold. I can die happy in the knowledge that my trust will be safely carried out. I knew I could depend upon you, boy of mine."

I kissed his hot brow and slipped the mysterious ring into my pocket as the old doctor clamored for admittance once more. That night my father passed out into the Great Beyond. He had gone forth upon his last Adventure.

CHAPTER TWO

THE SIGN OF THE DRAGON

THREE UNEVENTFUL YEARS had rolled by since the death of my father. Not so very long before he died, on my twenty-first birthday, to be specific, he had taken me into the business with him as junior partner, and the firm had changed from the widely known "Peter Brent" to "Brent & Son." Therefore, upon his demise, the supervision of the business came into my hands.

In order to be nearer my work I had disposed of the old place in Manorport, and taken apartments in Boston. Here I lived the life of a recluse. The ordinary social life of the city bored me tremendously. I still yearned for some outstanding adventure that I might look back upon in later years, and point to as having lifted me out of the rut of humdrum, everyday life. I had about come to the conclusion that adventure, as I interpreted the word, was dead. At any rate, I felt convinced it was not to be found outside the covers of some lurid fiction magazine. Adventure, however, is somewhat like a German submarine. She lurks in some unexpected quarter, waiting a chance to torpedo her victims without warning, and leaves them to sink or swim as best they may.

I had almost forgotten the dragon ring, which rested snugly at home in a corner of my desk drawer. The tale which had seemed so vivid at my father's telling, was losing its grip as they passed by. In fact, had it not been for an occasional "cleaning up" process, when I would always come across the odd ring he had given me, I think I would have forgotten the episode entirely.

At such time I would think over the whole story as he told it to me. I often wondered if the sign of the dragon would ever call upon me to keep the pledge my father made those long years before, and that I had sworn to observe.

I would always dismiss the matter with a laugh, and tuck the ring away once more, to be forgotten until the next time I "cleaned house." Of course, nothing would ever come of it! I was a fool to fritter away my time dreaming over such idle fancies. I was living in an age of science and system. Adventure was dead!

My longing for some sort of unusual happening made me weave romances around every odd character I passed upon the street. I built air-castles of adventure from the most trivial incidents. Somewhere I had read that each life was only one of a million "passing tales," that hidden in each life was some unsuspected incident that might furnish the material for a yarn such as few could spin. I wasted many idle moments in a futile endeavor to fathom the "skeleton in the closet" of my acquaintances and business associates.

Perhaps it was this trick of poking my nose into other people's business that accounted for the bad case of "nerves" I was developing. At twenty-five one ought not to shy at a shadow, as I confess I had been doing of late, especially when he was always prattling of an innate desire for adventure.

For the past few days I had the uncomfortable sensation of being followed. I could "feel" the intentness of a pair of eyes watching the back of my head. Wherever I went I had an uncontrollable desire to suddenly turn and confront whoever was on my trail.

Of course it was all absurd. Nothing more or less than a hallucination, due to my foolish imaginings.

Still, the feeling persisted with such bulldog tenacity I could not rid myself of it.

If any one was shadowing me I'll give them credit for making a good job out of it. Try as I might, I could not catch my shadow unawares. I tried every device I had ever read about for forcing one into revealing himself, but all to no avail.

The persistency of the notion gave me an uneasy feeling I can hardly describe. After a few days of it I decided to take a long postponed vacation. Then something occurred which startled me into a belief that perhaps adventure was still on the job, after all.

The morning mail arrived at my apartment each day just before breakfast, and part of my morning program, religiously adhered to, was the opening of the mail over the coffee cups.

There was always something, a bill from the tailor, an invitation to some function or other which would require a polite note of refusal; in fact, the tenor of my morning mail was quite often responsible for the frame of mind in which I reached the office.

This particular morning brought several letters. I glanced at them automatically before opening any of them, and my attention was arrested by one addressed in a distinctly feminine, yet unfamiliar hand.

I instinctively separated it from the others, and left it to be opened last.

There was the usual monthly statement from my club, and an advertisement or two that were quickly disposed of. With my usual habit of making a mountain out of a molehill, I began building a mystery right away around the unopened letter. Why should a young lady be writing to me? My acquaintances included few of the fair sex, and none who would have any reason for writing to me. (Of course, I imagined my unknown correspondent as young and, perhaps, a wee bit good looking.)

I turned the missive over and over in my hands, even holding it up to the light in a vain effort to get some inkling of the contents before I opened it. It was mine all right; there could be no mistake about that. The address was clear enough:

CHESTER BRENT, Esq.
Cheltingham Apartments, Boston, Mass.

I suppose if I had been anything but a hare-brained young fool, I would have had that letter opened and read two or three times, but as I have said before, I was a worshipper at the shrine of any possible adventure. At last I split the flap of the envelope, and drew out its contents expectantly. But with all my suppositions, I was totally unprepared for what that envelope actually contained. The note itself was unsigned, and was in the same firm, legible hand as the writing on the envelope.

It was short and businesslike in the extreme:

MY DEAR MR. BRENT:

I am very desirous of seeing you on a matter of importance. I take this method of announcing that I shall call at your office some time Tuesday, the twelfth, to interview you. As it is imperative that I see you in person, I shall identify myself by means of a card such as I have enclosed.

The note was puzzling enough, I'll admit, but it was not the note with which I was chiefly concerned. It was the enclosure. An ordinary-sized calling-card, perfectly blank except for a large blotch of red sealing wax in the center. And imprinted in the wax was an ensignia that could only have been made by the mate to the green dragon ring with the jade eyes, that reposed in my desk-drawer!

The sign of the dragon!

The words of my father came back to me as vividly as if he was at the moment speaking them again into my ear:

"…that Brent or Burgess, whichever the case might be, would respond to the sign of the dragon and render assistance to the limit of his ability and power."

And I was pledged to carry out this promise to the letter. I rescued my ring from its resting place and fitted it to the dragon seal upon the card. Any doubts that I might have had to its authenticity were immediately dispelled. It fitted as well as if my own ring had been the one to make the impression. My brain was whirling in an attempt to grasp the significance of it all. After all these years the twin rings were again fated to cross each other's paths. What would be the outcome?

I slipped the ring on my finger and gazed at it, fascinated by the gleaming jade eyes of the green and gold dragon. I rather hesitated to wear the ring, for I knew its oddity would invite innumerable questions, but I was resolved that it should accompany me wherever I went until this adventure was at an end. Tuesday the twelfth? That was tomorrow! I was keyed up to the highest pitch of excitement. Adventure was not dead! Without warning I had been plunged into what seemed to me must prove the experience I had wished for so long. A years-old pledge of fealty; twin rings of an oddity that defied adequate description as symbols of that pledge; an unsigned note in a feminine hand—what more could one ask in the way of a mysterious setting? I could have imagined nothing more promising of future thrills than this combination.

I don't exactly know how I got through the day, but I know that evening came at last. My mind was still intent upon the caller of the morrow. What would she be like? Would she be dark or fair, young or old? I pictured myself as the hero of all kinds of impossible adventures, with my mysterious correspondent as the much persecuted heroine. I slept but little that night, I can tell you, and my trip to the office was made with my mind way off somewhere above the clouds. Not another word had I heard. All that I knew was that the sign of the dragon had called to me to aid, and that the call had come in the handwriting of a woman.

CHAPTER THREE

ANITA BURGESS

MY EXPECTED VISITOR kept me on the anxious seat until well into the afternoon. For fear I might miss her, I pointed to a nearby restaurant and had them send my luncheon to the office. I was beginning to be assailed by doubts and misgivings, when the boy brought me an envelope addressed in the same handwriting as my note of the previous day. I knew before I opened it exactly what I would find inside. An exact duplicate of the card I already carried in my pocket. Just a blotch of red sealing wax, stamped with the sign of the dragon.

"Lady to see you, sir," he announced. "She wouldn't give her name, but she told me to bring you the note, and said you would understand."

"It's all right," I assented: "show her in."

The dragon ring in my pocket seemed to find its way to my finger automatically. At last my mysterious caller had arrived. At last I was to learn what service I could render to the owner of the other ring. I suppose I should have been calm and self-possessed, but my heart was beating at trip-hammer speed. I felt myself growing hot and cold by turns. As I rose to greet my visitor, however, I congratulated myself that outwardly I was as cool as a cucumber. My first impression of her was eminently satisfactory. From the top of her modish hat, set jauntily upon a wealth of auburn hair, to the tip of her natty gray kid boots, she was typical of the modern, self-reliant American woman. She was just the type that to my mind fitted her present role to perfection.

"Mr. Brent?" she inquired, extending her hand. I noticed at once, on the middle finger, a replica of the ring I was wearing. I nodded in acquiescence, and drew up a chair for her. "You received my note?"

In reply, I produced the two strange calling cards I had received.

"You have the advantage of me, Miss —"

"Burgess," she supplied. "Anita Burgess. I trust you will pardon the rather mysterious way in which I announced myself, but my business is of such a nature that I preferred my identity to remain unknown until I was sure I had found the right Mr. Brent."

"And you are certain?"

"Oh, yes. The ring on your left hand satisfies me on that score. But, to the business at hand. You are familiar with the pledge associated with the ring you wear?"

"I promised my father, on his death-bed, three years ago, to observe the pledge he made to your namesake, should the occasion ever arise."

"Good enough! I do not come to you through choice, Mr. Brent, but dire necessity. I have a favor to ask of you that may entail the risking of your life. I want you to listen closely to what I have to tell, and think carefully before you decide as to whether you wish to take so great a risk as I must ask of you."

I nodded.

"First of all, Mr. Brent, I want your promise that when I leave this building you will make no attempt to follow me, or to learn anything more of this affair than I choose to tell you."

"In other words, you are asking me to go into this affair with my eyes shut?"

"It is for your own protection as well as mine, Mr. Brent. From the time your connection with this matter is established, both your safety and mine are doubly menaced. I have exercised the utmost caution to keep my visit here this afternoon from reaching the ears of my—suppose I call them adversaries—and any act of yours that might tend to arouse their suspicions would set all my scheming at naught. Therefore, before I proceed, I would like your promise to make no move that might embarrass me or make my position more difficult."

"Very well, I shall abide by your wishes in the matter. Just what can I do to assist you?"

"I have in my possession certain documents that were left in my care by my father, who gave me the ring and told me its story at the same time. The nature of these documents I am not at present at liberty to divulge.

"There is a certain crowd that is very desirous of acquiring possession of these documents. The importance in which this other faction holds the acquisition of these papers will be emphasized when I tell you that two attempts have been made upon my life in the past few weeks. It was after the second attempt that I bethought myself of the pledge, connected with the odd ring that I had. I knew it could do no harm to look up the owner and see if he, too, held the pledge as sacred. If not, I would be no worse off than before; if he did, I would try to enlist his aid. My first step was to locate the Brents, whom my father had last heard of as still living in Manorport. I went there, and found that the Brent homestead had been sold, but that a Chester Brent, the son of the man my father knew, had moved to Boston, where he was carrying on his father's business. As I said before, all this information had to be gathered with the utmost caution, lest my opponents suspect I planned to enlist the aid of any one; and this made it doubly hard to procure. Luckily, I had but little difficulty in locating you, and here I am. Now, my plan is simply this: The very nature of these documents I speak of make them valueless unless one has the entire set of them."

Miss Burgess drew a sealed envelope from somewhere about her person, and laid it on the desk in front of me.

"In this envelope, sealed, are just half of the papers I mentioned. I have the other half in a duplicate package in my possession. Will you take charge of this package for me, with the solemn promise to guard it with your life, if necessary, until I send or come for it? Of course, you understand that I trust you to make no attempt to learn the contents. I may find it impossible to call for the package in person. Do not let it leave your possession on any pretext unless the one who demands it is wearing the ring I now wear."

"But suppose I am in doubt as to what move to make? I will not know where to locate you, or—"

"You have a phone at your apartment. I will communicate with you from time to time, when I can safely do so. You have my story, Mr. Brent. Think carefully before you make any decision. Remember that two attempts have already been made upon my life, and that, should your connection with this affair be established, your life, too, would be constantly in danger. It is no mere child's play, this undertaking, or I would not be tempted to enlist outside aid."

I picked up the sealed packet, and turned it idly in my hands. Prompted by some peculiar impulse, probably my inborn longing for adventure, I tucked it snugly away in my inside pocket.

"That is my answer, Miss Burgess. The package is now in my care. Rest assured that it will be ready for you when you desire."

"I fear, Mr. Brent," she went on, "that you underestimate the power of the forces that oppose us."

"I must remind you," I told her, "that you have asked me to help you because of the pledge made between my father and yours. Can I emphasize my seriousness more than by promising that, by the sign of the dragon ring, I shall protect these documents no matter to what risks or dangers I may be exposed?"

"My best wishes to you, Sir Knight of the Dragon," she smiled, rising. "Then I have your promise to make no effort to trace me or to ascertain the contents of that packet until I give you permission?"

"You have my promise," I solemnly returned.

With a last smile, the door closed behind her, and she was gone.

Alone once more, the whole conversation seemed more of a dream than anything else. It couldn't be possible, I told myself, that any such thing could happen here, in Boston, in the twentieth century. Impossible! And yet, the two unique calling cards were still on the desk before me, and I could feel the pressure of the package in my inside pocket to help convince me that it was not by any means a mere figment of my vivid imagination.

CHAPTER FOUR

THE EPISODE OF THE MYSTERIOUS STRANGER

YIELDING TO IMPULSE may some day get me into serious trouble.

When I promised Miss Burgess that I would make no attempt to locate her or learn any more about her than I already knew, I made it all in good faith. I would have undoubtedly kept it inviolate had it not been for a trifling incident that occurred a few evenings later.

I had not been to the theater for several weeks, and was determined to see a much-advertised play that was, according to its press agent, "the talk of the town."

I was rather disappointed in the performance. Not but what it was good enough in its way, but it didn't come up to my expectations, as is quite often the case with these over-advertised productions.

It was during the intermission between the second and last act that I spied her, directly ahead of me, just a few rows away.

There was no mistaking her for anyone else. Anita Burgess was of a distinctive type that one could pick out from among a thousand.

I thrilled at the thought that here was a girl whose life was constantly in danger and who was bold enough to attend a well-filled play-house, and alone! Perhaps, I decided, she was safer here than in her own home. One would scarcely attempt an assault where there were so many onlookers. Yes, her reasoning was correct; she was in no danger during the performance, at any rate.

But how about afterwards? I began to fancy all sorts of dangers besetting her. I wavered between my promise to keep away from her until I was sent for, and an asinine desire to play knight-errant, uninvited, and follow along at her heels to protect her.

The last act of the play was beginning, and I temporarily forgot the subject of Anita Burgess in my endeavors to find some redeeming feature in the play being enacted on the stage.

As soon as the play was ended and the lights flashed on, my mind reverted to the mystery girl and her problems again.

She had already risen, and was making her way along the crowded aisle, toward the foyer.

The idea of playing watch-dog to my lady of the ring must have gained a greater control over my mind than I imagined. For the moment my actions seemed to be regulated by some outside agency. I followed her down the aisle, keeping well in the rear, but always near enough so that I did not lose sight of her.

As she reached the foyer my attention was attracted to a man who detached himself from a small group of friends, broke off his conversation with an attractive olive-skinned young lady, and fell into step behind my quarry.

There was nothing unusual for an incident of this kind to happen in the crowded lobby of a theater, but a strange premonition warned me that this stranger was somehow connected with this affair.

He had every appearance of being a gentleman of the first water, and I could not find any logical reason for my suspicions. Still, I reflected, this affair to date had given me no indications as to whether I was arrayed against might of finance or physique.

We reached the street almost simultaneously, and it was with difficulty that I kept from being observed. Miss Burgess summoned a waiting taxi, and I turned my attention to the man whom I instinctively distrusted. He, too, had called a car. While I was not near enough to overhear his directions, I could gather from his gestures that he was instructing the driver to trail Miss Burgess' car. My impulses were leading me into an adventure with a vengeance. My suspicions regarding the stranger were not without foundation after all.

All my reluctance at the thought of breaking my promise to Miss Burgess fled with the increasing possibility of attendant danger. I was resolved, now, to follow on and see this thing through at all costs. I fretted and fumed as I waited for my machine to arrive. It would be all right, I decided, for me to indulge in this escapade. My chauffeur was discreet and would be willing to lend a hand, should I need him.

"Keep that other car in sight," I instructed, indicating the tail-lights of the receding automobile, "and keep out of sight yourself."

He nodded, and we sped along on the trail of the other machines. I hadn't the slightest idea where we were bound. I was still under the distinct impression that I could be of some service to the one who had summoned me at the call of the dragon ring. That was enough for me, all the incentive I needed to persuade me to follow on, irrespective of where the trail might lead. On we rode, until we had left the lights of Boston well behind. Finally I noticed that we were slowing down.

"The car ahead has stopped just this side of an old house up the line," the chauffeur told me through the tube. "I can see the taillights of another machine that's stopped directly in front of the house."

"Drive right on, past them both," I directed, "and when you get a way down the road, stop."

We passed the stranger's machine, which was drawn up at the side of the road. I could see that he was still inside. As we drew up to the house I strained my eyes to get a better view of things. It was well back from the road, and was flanked on either side by a heavy growth of underbrush and trees. I soon discovered the reason for the stranger remaining in his car. On the steps of the old mansion stood the trim figure of Miss Burgess, evidently waiting to be admitted. She must have dismissed her taxi, for the driver had turned and was heading his car towards the city. We drove along until we rounded a bend in the road, and the chauffeur brought the machine to a standstill.

Alighting and directing my man to wait until I returned. I picked my way cautiously back towards the old dwelling. I kept to the shadows as far as possible, as I neared my goal, but in spite of my caution I barely avoided a collision with the man I trailed as he emerged from the bushes just ahead. The auto that had brought him to the scene was no longer in sight. He seemed quite unaware that anyone might be following, and it proved an easy matter to observe his every move.

Fate must have directed my footsteps, for, while the stranger was constantly stepping upon dry, crackling twigs, or stumbling over loose stones, I had so far escaped them. A single misstep on my part would have been fatal.

With an ease born of long experience, the intruder noiselessly raised a window in the rear of the house. Silently he drew himself up, inch by inch, until his body was half over the sill, his legs left dangling awkwardly outside.

It was a case of now or never. Once he reached the inside of the house, I would be helpless to lend any assistance. With a single bound I was upon him. There was a crash and a shower of broken glass, as a flying fist crashed through the half-opened window. He lost his grip upon the sill, and we dropped to the ground together, his huge bulk nearly crushing the wind out of me.

In the moment's respite that followed my breathlessness, his hand darted out behind him and I saw the gleam of cold steel in the moonlight as his revolver flashed before my startled eyes. But I struck his wrist up just in the nick of time. A second later, and I would have been in a far, far distant land. The echo of the shot reverberated with enough volume to arouse the dead.

I had no time to speculate what was going on inside the house. I more than had my hands full with my opponent. He was a great deal heavier than I would have guessed, and lithe and wiry as a panther. As long as I could maintain my grip upon his wrist, the revolver was of no use to him, so I concentrated all my energy upon keeping the weapon out of harm's way. As I have hinted, my lucky star must have been in the ascendancy this night, for as we swayed to and fro, locked in a mighty embrace, he backed into the fallen trunk of a tree. In a twinkling I had thrown him, and in another the revolver was in my possession.

"Now get up!" I ordered peremptorily. "And be careful that you keep your distance. I would have no more compunction about shooting you than I would some mangy dog."

Then came the interruption.

"Just toss away that gun, if you please; then put your hands up above your head, and keep them there!"

It was the voice of Miss Burgess that rang out, authoritatively, behind me. I saw the stranger's hands shoot upwards, and, tossing my weapon in the direction of the voice I followed suit.

"Now, if you gentleman will be so kind as to step into the light, I would be interested to know what this is all about."

I turned, my hands still high above my head, and found myself looking into the muzzle of an efficient-looking thirty-two. It described an unwavering half-circle, covering both of us, and we followed Miss Burgess silently, as she made for the front of the house. As we stepped into the path, the light from the road made the scene as brilliant as if it were mid-day.

"Pray tell me what is the meaning of all this? Why, Mr. Brent, is it really you?" she interrupted. "There's no need for you to keep your hands up any longer. On second thought, you'd better go back and retrieve that revolver I made you throw away. I'll keep this other gentleman quiet until you return."

I did as she bade me, and came back quickly, to find their positions unchanged.

"How came you to get mixed up in this affair tonight, Mr. Brent?" she questioned.

I recounted all that had happened since I had first espied her in the theater.

"I apologize for breaking my agreement in regard to keeping away from you," I concluded, "but I felt that the circumstances justified me in following along."

"You have rendered me a service that quite offsets any rules you may have broken," she avowed. "There has been no harm done. I do not live here. My business at hand simply required that I make this trip tonight; that is all." Then turning: "Marion," she called to someone inside, "have you a few yards of clothes-line that I may use?"

In reply, a middle-aged woman appeared in the doorway, a coil of heavy rope in her hands.

"If you will get that for me, Mr. Brent"—then, as I returned, bearing the cord; to the stranger: "just put your hands behind your back, if you please. Remember, I can shoot as straight as anyone you ever knew, Mr. Man! Now, if you will tie his hands Mr. Brent— Thank you, ever so much. Once more I assure you that the service you rendered tonight is a very great one. I can handle this gentleman very nicely now. Goodnight Mr. Brent, until I see you again."

I took this as a dismissal and started down the path to where my car was waiting. As I turned into the road, I looked back just in time to see the mysterious stranger enter the house under the persuasive influence of Miss Burgess' revolver. She followed him, and the door closed behind them. I felt my newly acquired weapon nestling snugly in my hip pocket, and it was with quite a degree of assurance that I directed my driver to take me home.

CHAPTER FIVE

A THREAT AND AN INTRUSION

I HAD BEEN reckless enough to carry the packet of documents on my person since they had been entrusted to me. After the incident of the night before, I decided that it was quite necessary to procure a safer hiding place for them. The next question was where they could be hidden and yet be safe from prying eyes.

At last I hit upon the following scheme. At one of the places where the wall-paper overlapped, I loosened the paper with painstaking care. Then, even more carefully, I scraped away just enough of the plastering so that the packet would fit without causing the paper to bulge, yet not enough to allow it to slip down. A little flour and water paste, and the job was complete. I inspected the result and concluded that an expert would be unable to tell that anything had been tampered with. The ring remained to be concealed.

I turned a small tabourette upside down, and hollowed out enough of one of its legs to allow the admission of the ring. I fastened this in place with a double-headed tack. It was not as well hidden as the documents, but I was satisfied it was in a place where one would be unlikely to look for it, and I took the further precaution of utilizing the tabourette to hold a large pot of ferns that had adorned my center table. Next I cleared up the debris, and felt much relived, now that my charges were disposed of safely.

Quite naturally I was late in getting down to the office. As a matter of fact, I was barely in time to be on hand to receive an out-of-town buyer who was rated as one of the big customers of the firm. When a man is after big business he can scarcely stand on ceremony as to business hours. When R. F. Fitzgerald himself proposed that I dine with him that evening, I saw no other course open but to accept his invitation. By the time I got around to my routine work it was so far ahead of me it took me the biggest part of the day to get caught up. So it was that closing time came before I hardly realized it could be any later than mid-afternoon.

A hurried trip to my apartments, where I cleaned up a bit and changed my clothes, and I was off to meet Fitzgerald. Randolph Fitzgerald was one of the few really big men whose business required the raw materials that my firm handled. It was decidedly unusual for him to bother with the trade at all, his custom being generally to leave the details with his subordinates. So you see, the very presence of this man spoke of something in the wind. An invitation to dine with R. F. Fitzgerald was something to be coveted by one in my position.

It was a wonderful dinner. From a cocktail to demitasse it left nothing to be desired. R. F. punctuated the meal with an occasional reference to my father, whom he had known quite well, but for the most part the conversation was confined to commonplace.

It was not until the last of the dishes were cleared away and we were entrenched behind two big, black cigars that we settled down to business.

I put forth the best efforts of which I was capable, and before we had finished our first cigars I had written up an order so tremendously large that it staggered me. I knew it was by far the largest single order that had ever been written for the firm. At his suggestion we had gone up to his suite of rooms, and I was just about to light up my second cigar, when he rather jolted my visions of hooking the biggest fish I had had on my line.

"Brent," he purred, "before we consider this order as closed, there is a little matter I would like to discuss with you."

His attitude reminded me of a sleek, well-fed cat, who toys with a mouse she has captured just for the sake of seeing it struggle. I don't know just how I gained that impression, but I couldn't seem to banish the comparison from my mind.

"If it is a question of price, Mr. Fitzgerald, I assure you —"

"Tut-tut, my boy; you couldn't do better by me on price. No; it's something altogether different. You might say that it had no direct bearing on the business we have been discussing, but as the entire order hinges on it, I feel I can safely class it as part of the proposition."

I confess I was becoming sorely puzzled.

"I don't understand to what you refer."

"You will in a minute, Mr. Brent, if you'll give me a chance to explain. Listen to me. I know that you have in your possession a packet of papers that are absolutely worthless to you. I represent interests to whom those documents are all-important. We are prepared to leave no stone unturned in our efforts to acquire them, but first I wanted to give you an opportunity to turn them over to us of your own accord. My proposition is simply this: if you will turn that packet of documents over to me within the next twenty-four hours, the order that I have given you stands. Otherwise I will not only cancel it, but promise that I will use whatever influence I may have to turn trade in some other direction."

I was well-nigh stunned by this revelation. Truly, Miss Burgess had been right when she assured me that I greatly underestimated the forces against which I had pitted myself. I was stung to the quick by the offer that had just been made. It was nothing more or less than out-and-out bribery, and he had not even the grace to attempt to camouflage it in any way, shape or manner.

I might be tricked, but I was beyond the temptation of a bribe, alluring though the prize might be. I fully realized the effect on my business, should this man wield his tremendous power against me, but I was pledged by the sign of the dragon ring, and I would be loyal to my trust at any cost.

"What under the sun are you driving at? All this talk of mysterious papers and documents savors some movie serial plot. You sound like the villain in *Bertha, the Cloak Model*, or some such tommy-rot."

"It's no use for you to pretend ignorance of the affair, I can tell you, we know that you have those papers in your care." I rose with as much dignity as I could assume.

"You will pardon me for suggesting it, Mr. Fitzgerald, but I fear the wine you had with your dinner must have gone to your head. I had better bid you good-evening."

"As you wish, Brent." His tone hardened noticeably. "My offer still holds. You have twenty-four hours in which to make up your mind. Remember," he added, ominously, "should you choose to match your wits against ours, we have the power to crush you as one might crush an ant beneath his heel, and crush you we will!"

I left the hotel, my mind filled with all sorts of forebodings. My willingness to jump blindly into this affair, my abominable habit of yielding to my impulses, was due to prove more costly that I had ever realized.

Already I had incurred the enmity of one who was directly responsible for ten per cent of our annual business. A man with an influence far-reaching enough to sway another ten per cent whatever way he chose. I realized that his was no idle threat, and I mentally quavered as I pictured the business difficulties he had it in his power to make for me.

Not only that, but I had no way of knowing just what other powers he had lined up on this side. He had said that he represented 'interests' that would use any means, so long as they attained the ends they desired. I fear I shivered, involuntarily, as I tried to figure the magnitude of 'interests' that could use Rudolph Fitzgerald for an errand-boy.

But youth is optimistic, and I had not reached my apartments before this line of reckoning had given way to another. If a mere slip of a girl like Anita Burgess could see no reason why I, a descendent of a long line of pioneers and adventurers, would not be able to hold my own. I had wished for adventure, and now I was getting my wish, where could I find good cause to complain? I had worked myself into a much more cheerful frame of mind by the time I let myself into my apartments. But my none too tranquil nerves were due for yet another shock.

My rooms looked as if they had been visited by a desert sand-storm. They were a prize picture of chaos and disorder. Whoever my nocturnal visitor had been, he had attended to the task of ransacking my things with a thoroughness that bespoke worlds of experience at the job.

The floor around the desk was littered with letters and papers, the table-drawer was half-opened, its contents strewn recklessly over the place Chairs were overturned, pictures taken from their places on the wall, the bureau-drawers were open and my clothes were scattered in a tangled mess around the bed-room. Every article in the room had come in for its share of attention. The intruder had even gone so far as to slit the mattress on the bed in an attempt to locate what he sought.

In spite of the completeness of the upheaval, the packet of documents was still safely resting in its niche in the wall, and the ring remained un-found. I thanked my lucky stars that I had taken time to dispose of them in this way. A less carefully prepared hiding-place, and the package would surely have been among the missing.

A half-opened window and a convenient fire escape was enough to show how my place had been entered. I silently resolved to have a burglar alarm installed before the next day came to an end. I would take no more chances, rest assured of that, as this business was taking a decidedly serious aspect. It took me well into the night to put the room into any semblance of order, but the events of the evening had driven all thoughts of sleep from my mind.

I was handicapped by the oath of secrecy and I did not dare report this matter to the police because of the publicity that such a proceeding would entail. No, it was to be a battle of wits, and I must fight it alone.

But was I fighting it alone? I had gotten into the tangle to help Miss Burgess in her trouble, so by the same token why couldn't I count her as an ally? Her assistance might prove invaluable before this matter reached its culmination. The thought strengthened and stimulated me. The deeper I got into this matter, the higher my admiration rose for her courage. The incident of the night before commanded my attention, and I wondered what had occurred after I left the scene. What had gone on between the mysterious stranger and his fair captor? The more I puzzled over this affair, the further away I seemed to get from any adequate solution of the mystery that enshrouded the incident.

What was the nature of the documents in the packet in my keeping? Why should men of the caliber of R. F. Fitzgerald and his associates be so anxious to gain possession of it? What influence had drawn Anita Burgess as deeply into the affair? It was as complex as a Chinese puzzle. The dragon ring was leading me into a maze from which it was becoming increasingly difficult to extricate myself.

CHAPTER SIX

THE GIRL WITH THE DRAGON RING

COINCIDENCE was not responsible for a strikingly handsome girl being in the same restaurant as myself on the following day. She accounted for that sensation I had experienced of being followed from my apartments to the café. Of course, I had no suspicion that she had any business with me, until she came over and sat down at my table.

"Mr. Chester Brent?" she interrogated.

I sipped my coffee thoughtfully, and answered with a nod. The girl was an utter stranger, yet I had the distinct impression of having seen her somewhere before. The waiter appeared, and while she was ordering I took the opportunity to study her carefully. I instinctively assumed she was in some way connected with the dragon mystery (as I had begun to classify the chain of events in my own mind) and I waited for her to announce her purpose.

Perhaps she was an emissary from Fitzgerald. I had heard nothing from him all day, and the time allowed for my decision was practically at an end. If she was, I admired his choice. She was a decided brunette, dark-skinned, with carefully moulded features. Indeed, the olive tint of her skin and a slight accent when she addressed me, conveyed the impression that she was of foreign extraction. The waiter hurried off to fill her order, and she directed her attention to me again.

"I have heard of you, Mr. Brent. I came in here to dine tonight, and it is so extremely lonely, dining alone, don't you think so? I saw you, also alone, and took the liberty of joining you. I hope you are not offended?"

"Not in the least," I parried. I knew there was some deeper motive in her action than a mere desire for companionship. I was slightly disappointed that she had not offered some more plausible excuse to defend her move.

Her eyes narrowed, and she eyed me piercingly, as though to determine my seriousness. The scrutiny must have satisfied her, for she went on:

"That is fine. We shall have a delightful dinner together." "And afterwards?"

"We shall let afterwards shape its own course, shall we not, Mr. Brent?"

She toyed with one of the forks, drumming idly with it on the edge of the table. Was it merely a trick of my imagination, or did that tap-tap-tapping of the fork resolve itself into measured beats and pauses, some sort of pre-arranged signaling? Nonsense; of course not! The sound would not carry twenty feet away, and the adjoining tables were unoccupied.

"As you choose. I only anticipated a pleasurable evening in your company, unless, of course, you have other plans."

She hesitated.

"No, not exactly that. After all, I could spend my evening in much less desirable company."

It was my turn to pause. I gazed at her intently until politeness forced me to remove my eyes from hers, but I could detect nothing except mere banter in either her tones or manner.

"Thank you. With such an unconventional beginning everything certainly seems most propitious for a rather unusual evening."

I don't know whether it was the remark or the arrival of the waiter that silenced her. When she spoke again her attitude had changed.

"Do you know, Mr. Brent, I have heard a great deal about you lately."

"Really? What, pray tell, has been the reason for my sudden popularity? Or is it some sort of notoriety instead?"

"Perhaps neither. It happens, sometimes, that a friend may speak well of one to an equally close friend, you know."

That remark left me rather up in the air.

"And that mutual friend?"

"From what I have heard your circle of those you count as friends is not so large but what you should easily guess."

I confess she was proving more of a match for me, but I did not dare venture to volunteer too much information until I understood her connection in this tangle.

When I lapsed into silence she regarded me with her lips curling into an amused smile, and the meal continued in absolute silence. I ventured to think that her desire for companionship was easily satisfied, but wisely kept my thoughts to myself and waited for her to make the next move.

"Your attitude during dinner reminds me of a turtle," she told me as the meal drew to a close.

"In what way?"

"Why when a turtle tires of his associates he simply draws up into his shell and stays there."

"My silence you mean?" and she nodded. "It was simply a case of not being able to think of anything that might interest you. By the way, now that dinner is nearly through, what next?"

"I have a somewhat unconventional favor to ask of you." Now it was coming. I had known all along her flimsy claim of lonesomeness was crude camouflage.

"I make no rash promises."

"It is just this, Mr. Brent. There is a little matter I wish to discuss with you, but I wish to be sure that I am safely sheltered from prying eyes and ears. I wonder if you could take me to your apartments? We would be perfectly safe there."

"Perhaps we would and perhaps we wouldn't. Bachelor apartments are hardly the place to entertain an unchaperoned young lady. It would be a case of smuggle you in and smuggle you out, and should you be discovered there would be the very devil to pay."

"I am prepared to meet just such a contingency as you mention. I quite agree that a young lady such as myself could hardly expect to visit a gentleman's apartments alone and at night. But a young man—a boy? Surely, there could be no objections to your bringing home a young male friend?"

"Then you mean —"

"You get my idea exactly; I mean that I shall accompany you to your rooms, but dressed as a boy. It is feasible, even though it is a trifle out of the ordinary. There we can talk things over freely."

She marked my reluctance to decide, opened her bag and took out a card, which she dropped on the table in front of me. I looked down upon the now familiar red seal, marked with the insignia of the dragon, and my hesitancy vanished in a flash.

"As you desire," I assented, "if you think the plan can be carried out successfully."

"I haven't the slightest doubt of it. First I must trouble you to take me to Boule's. As you are probably aware, he is a costumer—rents fancy costumes for masquerades and such things, you know."

I paid the waiter, summoned a waiting taxi, and in a few minutes we drew up to the front of Boule's.

She asked me to wait in the taxi until she returned, and it seemed scarcely a quarter hour when she was again beside me in the machine. The change was so complete that I hardly knew her myself for the charming young lady who had left me such a short time before. As a boy she was even more prepossessing than she was as a girl, and she had told the truth when she said she was prepared for this move. Everything must have been laid out for her in anticipation of just such a procedure. No one, in the semidarkness of the evening, could ever have detected that she was not the young man she was supposed to be.

Again that feeling swept over me that I had seen her somewhere before, but I brushed it lightly aside and wondered what message Miss Burgess was sending by this stranger, and why she had been unable to deliver it in person.

"You look great," I told my new-found "gentleman friend." "You'd pass muster anywhere."

She smiled.

"Many difficulties are easily surmounted, Mr. Brent. When one is prepared to cope with them. It was necessary that I make this trip to your apartments, therefore it was equally necessary that I be prepared to make it in safety."

"But suppose I had refused to countenance your proposition?"

"Then I was prepared to use this leverage to overbalance your objections."

There, gleaming in the palm of her hand, was the dragon ring I had last seen on the finger of Anita Burgess. My friend was not lacking in credentials; first the card, then the ring itself. We arrived at the apartments without incident, and made our way up the stairs.

"You will have to excuse the appearance of the place," I apologized as we entered, "but I had a surreptitious visitor last evening, who nearly wrecked the place, and I haven't had ample opportunity to straighten things out as yet."

"You mean that your rooms were broken into?"

"Exactly." I told her of the condition of the room upon my return the night before, concluding: "But they didn't succeed in finding the articles I have reason to believe was the sole object of the intrusion."

"Then they are still safe?"

"You mean the documents? Yes. As safe as when I first took charge of them."

Under the bright lights of the electric bulbs my "boy" visitor looked doubly attractive. Her well-rounded figure and dark skin and eyes fitted her new role to perfection. I saw her eyes glisten as I mentioned the papers.

"I'm so glad they are safe. I feared, when you spoke of the attempted robbery, that they had succeeded in getting them away from you."

"No; I had them safely hidden. Now, may I ask what business brings you here to-night that could not be transacted outside of my rooms?"

"I came for that package we have just been talking about."

I remembered Miss Burgess' instructions: "I may find it impossible to call you for the package in person. Do not let it leave your possession on any pretext, unless the one who demands it is wearing the ring I now wear," and the claimant had not only produced the ring, but one of those odd cards with which Miss Burgess had twice presented me.

"I don't quite see the necessity of this masquerade. Why not have had me deliver the package to you at some point outside?"

"Because I will not be suspected of acting as intermediary in this affair, whereas, if you attempted to carry it on your person there would be danger of its falling into other hands."

"Do you happen to know what disposal is to be made of it?" I wanted to be absolutely certain that I was doing right before I relinquished it. I couldn't rid myself of that sense that of uncertainty that had swept over me at the idea of giving this girl the packet, although she had the dragon ring, and I could think of no reason for doubting her. Of course, the incident had been out of the ordinary, but, for that matter, so had the whole affair.

"Only that I am to take it directly to headquarters," she replied.

I decided everything must be O.K. I could harbor no further doubts but what Miss Burgess had sent her for the documents. I would deliver them into her keeping, and my visitor watched me interestedly as I loosened the wall-paper and drew the packet from its hiding-place.

"Cleverly done, Mr. Brent," she complimented me. "No wonder your intruder failed to locate them."

"It seemed to baffle him just a little."

The jangle of the telephone in the next room interrupted me. The phone was on a stand near enough to the bed to make it handy if I had any night calls.

I thrust the packet of papers into my pocket.

"If you will pardon me for just a moment?"

"Surely. Run right along."

I vanished into the bed-room and snatched the receiver from the hook, savagely.

As I listened to the voice that came over the wire, my manner changed. I listened breathlessly, intent on catching every word.

"Is Mr. Chester Brent there?"

"This is Mr. Brent speaking."

"This is Miss Burgess, Anita Burgess," the voice went on.

"I have been trying to get in touch with you all evening. Do not let those documents get out of your hands one single instant until I can see you again. My dragon ring—the one my father gave me, you know, has been stolen!"

CHAPTER SEVEN

INTO THE LION'S DEN

MISS BURGESS' conversation came to an abrupt termination when I heard the clink of the receiver as it fell into place at the other end of the wire. The message had so startled me that I stood rooted to the spot, the receiver still held to my ear, until the operator's "Number, please," roused me to action.

The warning had arrived just in time, for a few moments later damage would have been done. The imposter in the other room would have gained her objective—the documents entrusted to me would have been irretrievably lost. I shuddered as I realized how nearly I had made the fatal mistake of giving her the bundle.

A sudden flash of recognition, and I knew where I had previously encountered the masquerader. She was the young lady with whom my mysterious stranger of two evenings before had been talking when I had first noticed him in the foyer of the theatre.

I mentally cursed myself as several varieties of idiot for not having remembered her at sight. Still it had been only a fleeting glimpse of her, so perhaps I was not altogether to blame. Simultaneously a more sinister thought occupied my attention. The legend connected with the ring came back to me. "Should one of the rings be stolen, the charm gave way to a curse, and sudden death would assuredly be meted out to the perpetrator." I thought of the two incidences in which I knew of the working out of the superstition, and I wondered which one of us was to be the victim. The thought of this dark-haired beauty coming to an untimely end was most disconcerting, even though she was one of the elements of danger I was facing.

Thoughts travel fast, and all this had taken but a mere fraction of the time it takes to tell it. Since the fight at the country home I had carried the revolver that I had then acquired, and the feel of it, as my hand stole intuitively to my pocket, reassured me. I felt myself equal to any situation that might arise. It was evident that the girl's suspicions were not aroused. She was still in the big chair where I had left her, looking over a copy of some magazine she had chosen from the stand. My first precaution was to cross the room, placing myself so as to be between the girl and the door.

"Nothing of any importance," I told her. "Just someone with time to kill and a telephone handy. I pleaded important business, and we rang off."

"Then suppose we get back to the matter at hand," she suggested. "It is getting rather late, and I should be going. If I may have that package —"

She paused abruptly. I had backed to the door, and the sound of the tumblers in the lock as I turned the key, surprised her. Then she rose, her eyes flashing dangerously.

"Exactly what do you mean by doing that, Mr. Brent?"

I took the key from the lock and put in my pocket before I replied.

"It means, my unknown friend, that it is my turn to do a little dictating. I would thank you to hand over that dragon ring that was stolen earlier in the evening."

She drew herself stiffly erect. Her black eyes narrowed until they were mere slits. Instantly she was on the defensive. There was no trace of fear, no hint of timidity in her manner. I could almost picture, in her stead, a tawny panther at bay, crouched ready for a final spring upon those who sought to destroy her.

"Do you mean to imply that I —"

"I mean to imply nothing; I mean to accuse. The owner of that ring has just informed me of its theft. The ring is in your possession. I can draw but one logical conclusion."

"So that was the nature of your unconsequential telephone call?"

"Your power of intellect does you credit, my fair friend." Again her eyes flashed belligerently.

"It is quite possible that I might refuse to comply with your request."

"As a lever, cold steel is often quite effective as a talisman." She did not even quiver as she found herself looking down the barrel of my weapon, and said cooly:

"Granted. In some cases a more powerful leverage is required than others, Mr. Brent. Are you quite sure your particular lever is equal to the task?"

She was slowly retreating in the direction of the window that opened onto the fire escape.

"I think it would be more conducive to your welfare if you didn't exhibit such a roving tendency. I think you had better be seated. Your familiarity with the exits here leads me to believe that perhaps you may have seen these apartments before."

She took the chair I indicated before she parried·

"It is my turn to congratulate you upon your keenness of intellect."

So here was my intruder of the night before! In spite of the fact that she was aligned against me, I could not help but feel a growing admiration for her prowess and courage.

"It might interest you to know that since your previous visit I have taken the precaution to install the protection of a burglar alarm. Another such attempt would only succeed in arousing the household."

"Since your previous visit," she mimicked, with a tantalizing smile. "My, but don't we take a lot for granted this evening. And aren't we progressive. I should apply to you for lessons in locking the barn door after the horse has been stolen."

Her banter was goading me to distraction. My rising anger must have reflected in my expression, for she laughed heartily.

"But in this case the 'horse' wasn't stolen," I reminded her.

"True enough, although it nearly got out of the stable in spite of your elaborate system of 'alarms.' They didn't succeed in keeping me out after all, you see."

"I still have the package." I inwardly regretted that its hiding place was revealed. Should a future opportunity be afforded for a search of the apartments, I feared I could devise no place of concealment where I would feel it was safely disposed of. "Once more I must ask you to give me that ring."

"Suppose I should scream?" she suggested. "If I remember rightly, it was you who mentioned that bachelor apartments were hardly the place for a young lady to be found, alone, at this hour."

"Then I should be forced to the unpleasant necessity of turning you over to the authorities. Sneak-thieves are not uncommon in apartment houses, and the fact that you are in boy's clothes precludes the possibility of your being able to offer a logical alibi."

I had drawn up a chair, and sat facing her, being careful to keep the drop upon her. Behind her banter I sensed her desperation and I knew that, should the slightest opportunity present itself, she would stake her all in a wild attempt to regain her freedom. It was my turn to take the initiative.

"Might I suggest that all this talk is getting us nowhere? Don't you think you might just as well hand over that ring now? Thank you. I felt sure you would see the wisdom of it sooner or later."

She glared at me vindictively as the ring changed hands. "What is it pleasure to do with me? It is highly improbable that you intend to detain me here all night."

"Quite true. It is also highly improbable that I shall turn you loose to set Lord only knows how many cut-throats after my life before morning."

"You have your burglar alarms, ironically."

"And just at present I have you, which I consider a hundred-fold more protection than all the burglar alarms in the world."

"May I inquire what use the captor intends to make of the prisoner?"

"You may. I was about to tell you, anyway. I understood you to say that your intentions were to take this package," I tapped my pocket significantly, "direct to headquarters,"

"Those were my instructions."

"Suppose, then that you obey those instructions. I would hate to be the one to stand in the way of so admirable a young lady's execution of the task entrusted to her Of course, it will be wiser if they remain in my possession in transit. You see, my fair unknown, I have rather a strong inclination to find out just where the 'headquarters' you spoke of might be."

"You would dare?"

"Why not? When my own rooms are not safe from intrusion, I figure I will be just as secure elsewhere, and you will agree with me, I am sure, that to do the unexpected always gives one a decided advantage; for example, your visit here this evening. I confess, had it not been for that telephoned warning, you would have accomplished your mission with the utmost ease."

"If you insist, Mr. Brent, I suppose I have no other course to pursue. I warn you, fairly and squarely, that you will regret forcing me into doing this thing."

I suppose I was foolhardy in the extreme to propose such a venture. Walking boldly into the lion's den is by no means likely to prove to be a bed of roses. But I was riled. The gullibility with which I had walked into the trap set for me, and the narrowness of my escape, stung me into a rashness that allowed of no prudence or caution.

"I shall have to ask you to step into the other room with me while I telephone for a taxi."

She silently obeyed. I placed her advantageously in front of me while I called up the taxi-cab office and ordered a car sent up immediately.

Getting into my top-coat and still maintaining the advantage the revolver afforded me was quite a task. I was painfully awkward about it, but the main thing is that I accomplished it without mishap. Then I concealed the revolver in the outside right-hand pocket of the ulster, but still kept it to bear upon my captive.

"Remember," I cautioned her, "although this revolver is out of sight, I can shoot as well through the cloth of this coat as if it was not in the way. While I would regret shooting at a woman, if the necessity should arise—"

The significance of the pause was not lost upon her.

"You can threaten rather melodramatically, I am sure," she proclaimed. "What, pray, must I do to avoid the sensation of a bullet in my brain—though my capture leads me to doubt if I have one."

"Simply take me back, or let me take you back, to 'headquarters.' As I suggested before, I am anxious to learn more about your superiors in this matter. You interest me only as a means to that end. It is the men higher up who commend my attention."

I suppose the remark was rather brutal. If looks would kill, the one she flashed me would have sealed my doom. As it was, I dreaded the consequences should she succeed in regaining the upper hand. Wound a woman in body or in soul and chances are equal that you may be forgiven; wound her pride and she will seek vengeance for the rest of her days.

"Bear in mind that if I even so much as suspect you of double-crossing me, your apparent freedom will be at an end."

I had transferred the all-important package to the inside pocket of my suit-coat. I felt that it was as safe there as it would be left unconcealed about the rooms. I had also appropriated several yards of heavy cord on the chance that it might be of some use before the night was over. Then the taxi arrived, and my prisoner in the lead, we descended the stairs.

The address she gave the chauffeur surprised me. It was in one of the most exclusive sections of the city.

Once inside the machine she lapsed into sullen taciturnity. Night rides, I reflected, were becoming a habit. We drew up in front of an imposing residence which bore all the earmarks of being closed for an indefinite period. The windows were boarded, the lawn was unkempt and neglected, the grounds were shrouded in absolute darkness. The general effect was that of some cold, dead thing. No sign of life was visible. A starless, overcast sky, that gave promise of an approaching storm, lent added solemnity to the scene. I paid the driver, and we watched the lights of the receding machine vanish into the darkness.

"The main task that confronts you, young lady, is to arrange things so that I can see and hear all that goes on without being seen or heard myself. Is this the place?"

She chose to maintain her attitude of silence, and replied with an answering nod.

I felt like a maurader as I followed her into the pitch-black darkness of the grounds. Lest she find some chance to elude me in the darkness, I held to her coat-tails with my free hand much as a blind man would cling to his leader for guidance and protection. The other hand still kept its grip upon the revolver that bulged in my pocket until we reached a side entrance to the dwelling, and the girl produced a key which she fitted to the lock. I drew the weapon from under cover. If I was going into this darkened house I would be prepared for emergencies.

"Follow me closely," she whispered as we stepped into the inky blackness of the hallway. "Perhaps you had best keep hold on my coat."

"I will be right at your heels and so will this." I prodded her with the muzzle of my revolver and trailed her through three or four spacious rooms, lighted only by an occasional moonbeam that found its way through the apertures in the boarded-up windows. She steered me deftly around the dust-laden furniture without bumping against anything. It gave me an eerie feeling, this owl-like ability of hers to see in the dark. My own eyes were becoming used to the dense darkness, and I could begin to distinguish the objects we passed more clearly.

We were making our way towards the center of the mansion. At last a light gleamed from behind drawn portieres. A tug at her coat checked the speed of my leader, but the caution was needless. The room though brilliantly lighted, was empty. I noticed the spick and span cleanliness of the room, in striking contrast to the dusty, musty unused apartments we had passed through in reaching it. Its luxurious furnishings were well in keeping with the house itself; heavy draperies at the windows and doors, thick carpets that rendered our steps noiseless, well appointed furniture. Whoever owned them was not only wealthy, but was possessed of marvelously good taste in his selections. All in all, the room was a study in harmony.

"The man I expected to meet here has evidently not arrived," the girl volunteered, sinking into a comfortable looking rocker.

"Then we shall wait for him," I said, preparing to take my place opposite.

A moment later the sound of a closing door brought me to my feet again.

"That must be him now," she whispered.

The room opened into another that was as dark as the rest of the house had been, and I drew the heavy draperies across the doorway muttering:

"Behind these curtains I can observe all that is going on. Any inkling that I am here, or any false move on your part will prove your undoing." I retreated to the protection of the draperies as the sound of approaching footsteps fell upon our ears. Nearer and nearer they came until I knew their owner must be directly outside the room where the girl lay idly in her chair.

The curtains at the other end of the room parted, and a man steeped into the light. He was the same one I had first seen her talking with in the theater; the mysterious stranger whose hands I had tied and left at the mercies of Anita Burgess at the house in the country two nights before.

CHAPTER EIGHT

THE CURSE OF THE RING

THE MAN SWEPT the room with one comprehensive glance, took in the figure of the erstwhile boy in the rocker, and gave vent to his feelings with a low whistle.

"You're some sketch in that rig, Julia, believe me."

She gave him an icy stare.

"'Miss Sabastino,' if you please."

"'As you like it,' as the old bard would say."

I sensed a feeling of animosity between them. It was evident from the man's attitude that he was in a position to give the girl orders, but her whole demeanor spoke of forced obedience. He converted the end of the table into a seat, and one foot beat a soundless tattoo upon the carpeted floor.

"Did you get my instructions this afternoon?"

"I wouldn't otherwise be here in this outlandish get-up," she flared.

Methodically he opened his cigarette case, selected one with care, lighted it without asking her permission, and blew several rings of blue smoke ceiling ward before he continued:

"Did you meet with any degree of success last evening?"

"Don't talk to me of success," she snapped. "It's bad enough for me to have to do your dirty work without listening to your sarcasms. I waited here till nearly sunrise to report on last night's venture, but you couldn't even let me know you were not going to meet me. Bah!"

He waved his hand in an eloquent gesture.

"My dear lady, if you had been in my predicament last evening, I doubt if even you would have been able to send any communications."

"You interest me. What was the dire calamity that befell you?"

"I had the somewhat doubtful pleasure of spending the night trussed up like a sack of potatoes. In fact, the night before and all of yesterday as well."

"I am surprised to think that a man of your much vaunted abilities should submit to such ignominious treatment!"

He swung angrily from the table and strode menacingly toward her.

"Damn you! Some day you'll rile me to a point where I shall kill you!"

The girl laughed tauntingly.

"But not so long as you have need of my services, signor. Come, calm yourself. Can't you see I can hardly wait to hear what you have been doing since you ran away from me in the theater?"

I was wondering if she was really so desirous of learning what had happened, or whether she was drawing him out for my benefit. His anger passed as suddenly as it has risen, and he resumed his perch on the corner of the table. Then he sketched for her, briefly, his activities from the time I had left him facing Miss Burgess' revolver in the light from the road.

"Everything would have been as easy as rolling off a log if it hadn't been for the interference of that young pup Brent."

My blood boiled at this insult and my muscles tensed in silent rage, but I controlled myself with an effort, and listened as the girl queried:

"You let the Burgess girl take you inside?"

"I had little choice in the matter. Far be it from me to invite anyone to indulge in target practice, with yours truly as the target. She took me up to an attic room, and between the two women had me hog-tied like a steer. That Burgess girl, the young demon, tried to make me talk. You can guess how well she made out. She threatened all kinds of terrible punishments and tortures if I insisted on keeping silent, but that didn't worry me much. When it comes right down to brass tacks, a women is too squeamish and chicken-hearted to carry out her threats. So I stoutly refused to talk." His features twisted into a wry smile as he added: "They weren't very merciful about the way they tied me up. I haven't worked all the soreness out of my joints yet."

"But how did you manage to get away?"

"Oh, that part of it was easy enough, once the chance came. I had to eat, you know, and at meal times I had the delightful pleasure of Miss Burgess' companionship plus her revolver, while the other women attended to loosening my hands and tying them up again. Yesterday noon the girl must have been out somewheres, and the old women made the mistake of thinking she could manage me alone. Once my hands were free, the rest was simplicity itself. I overpowered her before she could make a sound. Oh, I didn't harm her," as a look of concern registered on the Italian girl's countenance, "I just tied her up as I had been, and left her there."

"My legs had been tied for so long that it was several minutes before I could use them. Then I went a-searching for whatever I might find. My supposition regarding the girl was a correct one. Except for the old women upstairs the house was deserted. It was my turn to play in luck. On the table in one of the rooms downstairs I made a rare find. My capture must have made Miss Burgess careless in the extreme. She had gone off and left her handbag behind, and in that handbag I found the dragon ring and the cards I sent you."

So the girl was not the thief at all! The curse associated with the theft of the ring came back to me for the second time that night, and with it an inward relief that its working portended evil for someone beside the girl.

"I knew the value of my find, the new power the possession of this talisman gave me. The boss had told me of the significance of the dragon ring. In my hands, my find was useless. Brent knew me now as being lined up against him, so that as far as openly approaching him was concerned, my hands were tied. So I thought of you at once. You were unknown to him. In your hands the ring might be of intrinsic value. My next problem was to get them to you, with some sort of instruction for using them, before their loss was discovered. I set off down the road, bent on finding some town or village where I could communicate with the boss. It couldn't have been more than a mile and a half to the nearest town, but that last half- mile was torture. My muscles rebelled at the task put upon them after their enforced vacation. The boss had a nice, hot, ready-made panning out to give me, but when I told him about finding the ring it sort of sweetened his temper. He told me about you falling down on your job last night, too. I only asked you to see what you'd have to say about it."

"After I'd entirely given you up," said the girl, "I phoned him at the number you gave me. I nearly wrecked the place, too, but not a packet of documents could I find. I'd liked to have seen that fellow's face when he got a look at the place. I certainly messed things up for him."

Beyond a doubt, she had. The man continued:

"The boss told me where I could reach you, but said that I'd better not try to see you in person, lest we be seen together by Brent or the girl. He told me to send you the cards and ring by messenger, and that he would instruct you in your part over the telephone."

As he talked the stranger smoked incessantly. All the windows were tightly closed, and the room was slowly filling with a blue, smoky haze. Gradually the rings of smoke drifted behind the draperies where I was concealed. The smoke alone would not have done it, but, combined as it was with the close, musty atmosphere of the unused room, I felt a growing, irrepressible desire to sneeze. The girl had not moved in her chair, except to draw one knee up between her clasped hands while she gave rapt attention to the stranger's tale.

"Yes, I received both the ring and the instructions. To a certain point they worked to perfection."

"Up 'to a certain point,'" he sneered. "You don't mean to tell me that—"

I could not hold it back any longer. It was more than mere human nature could stand. I made an ineffectual attempt to smother it behind my hand.

"Ca-choo!"

The stranger bounded from the table as if shot from a cannon.

"What was that?" he fired the question at the girl.

Her faced blanched white as snow and she shrank away from him as though she would like to merge herself with the upholstery of the chair she occupied, and recovered her poise almost instantly, but not before a lurking suspicion crossed his mind.

"How do you suppose I know?"

He gripped her arm and pulled her bodily from the chair. "Rollo Bassino," she panted, "take your hand off my arm! Let me go at once! Let me go, do you hear?"

She winced as his grip tightened.

"I'll let you go when I get damned good and ready! Are you going to tell me who is hidden in that room or must I find out for myself? Is it some lover you have been meeting secretly, or some spy your treachery has allowed to take his place among us?" Her face flushed hotly at his accusations.

"Very well then, find out for yourself—if you can. You wouldn't believe me if I told you,"

With an oath he literally flung the girl aside. Under the impetus she staggered drunkenly across the room and brought up against the further wall. The jar dislodged a large hanging minor, and it tumbled to the floor with a tremendous crash, the glass splintering into a thousand fragments.

He was crossing the room towards my hiding-place with tremendous strides. I steeled myself for the encounter that I knew was inevitable, and it struck me as rather a trick of Fate that I was armed with the same weapon I had taken from him two nights ago. I caught the reflection of light upon the automatic in his hand, and knew he had replaced his loss at the first opportunity.

If it was to be fight, I had every advantage on my side. From my location in the darkened room I could watch his every move, while he only knew somewhere in the dark I was lying await for him. While I knew that he was armed he had no way of knowing whether I was or not. It remained for the girl to discount my superiority. I had forgotten her in my endeavor to keep an eye on the man, whose eyes gleamed insanely in the brilliant light of the room. Unseen, she made her way along the wall of the room. With one quick motion she threw aside the protecting draperies, and I stood revealed.

If I could help it, I didn't want to injure this man. If I could capture him unharmed, I would be in a fair way to gain some information I very much desired. I was quite handy with a revolver, and determined on attempting to shoot the automatic from the hand of the other man. If I should succeed, the rest would be comparatively easy. The girl I knew to be unarmed, and could I manage to disarm the man, I felt that I would be master of the situation. If I failed —

My finger tightened on the trigger as Bassino's gun came up into position. Again the girl changed the entire situation. As the hammer of the pistol shot home, she flung at me a small, half-filled goldfish globe in an effort to deflect my aim. Her move was fatal for the man. The glancing blow, as the globe grazed my shoulder, was just enough to change the course of the bullet, but not enough to save the man who opposed me. Instead of shooting the weapon from his hand, as I intended, the bullet chose a course straight as a die for the breast of the victim.

So quickly was the whole scene enacted, that he did not even have a chance to press the trigger. He stopped in his tracks, his fingers slowly relaxed, the automatic slipping through his nerveless fingers. He clutched at the wound, from which a tiny trickle of blood was already seeping. A few staggering steps forward, and he crumpled in a lifeless heap at my feet. Once more the curse of the dragon had been fulfilled.

CHAPTER NINE

ANITA TAKES A HAND

THE REALIZATION that I had shot the fellow being at my feet appalled me. True, I had only intended to disarm, at the most disable him; nevertheless, the fact remained that he was dead—that he had come to his death by my hand.

I gazed at the still smoking revolver in my hand; then, down at the inert form of the stranger I had mur— No, no not that! Killed in self-defense was better. I was dazed, overwhelmed with the enormity of my deed. The lethargy into which my self-introspection had plunged me proved my undoing.

Not for a moment had Julia Sabastino lost her self-possession. Bassino's automatic had scarce touched the floor when she thought to procure it. I came out of the stupor to find myself facing a determined looking pistol, behind which was an equally determined girl.

"I think the tables are turned once more," she said. "Just drop that gun before you do some more damage."

Had she but known it, she could have taken it from me without the slightest resistance. I was entirely unnerved. For the moment my longing for adventure had departed absolutely. As a bad, bold, brave adventurer I was worth considerably less than a plugged nickel. Where was all the resourcefulness, the ability to extricate oneself from all sorts of pitfalls, that was supposed to be part and parcel of every hero's make-up? I fear I made a sorry hero. Given long, pointed ears and a tail, I could easily have been mistaken for a jackass. Recent events had followed one another in such bewildering confusion that my power to adjust myself to the kaleidoscopic conditions had been utterly exhausted. And to cap the climax I had killed a man!

For the time being I was an automation, subject to the control of any will stronger than my own. I relinquished the revolver not because of any conscious effort on my part simply because the girl had willed me to drop it. I was in a state of self-imposed hypnosis, my mind dominated by Miss Sabastino's.

"Now, if you will back up a few steps while I obtain that gun. I'm taking no chances this time," the girl went on, coldly.

My action brought me to the edge of the darkened area behind me. Had I been in the possession of normal faculties, I might have risked a dash for liberty into the unused portion of the house, trusting to luck to find some safe means of egress. As it was, I paused while she disposed of my weapon, previously the dead man's (I shuddered at the thought), by tucking it into the pocket of her coat.

"For the last time, Mr. Brent, I will ask you for those documents. I trust you will not have the heart to refuse me."

I handed them over as submissively as a punished child. In anticipation of her next request I extended the dragon ring.

"No, thank you." Her tone was bittersweet. "I do not need your passport now that I have these." She flaunted the documents tauntingly before my eyes. "That rope you brought with you was a happy thought, indeed. I doubt if I could have located any handy enough to be of any value. Must I ask you for it a second time? Oh, thank you. There is a nice convenient, straight-back chair, Mr. Brent. You must be tired after standing for so long a time. My, my how quickly you gather my meaning. We are getting on famously together, aren't we? Steady just a moment now, while I fasten these knots securely. Well done is twice done, so they say."

She had been deftly tying me to the chair as she talked, and when she finished I could not move a muscle.

"I see no need of adding to your difficulties by gagging you. If you should scream I'm sure the sound would not penetrate to the street. I dislike the thoughts of leaving you all alone, but I fear that I must. If you get lonely, think of me. Your anger may dispel your lonesomeness. Now that he is out of the running"—at the reference to him her voice tinged with bitter scorn—"I suppose I've got to do his work as well and take these to the boss. If you don't liberate yourself before morning I promise to be generous and come back and set you free. Now I must bid you adieu."

I heard her receding footsteps and the slam of the door behind her. It was raining. The storm the cloudy sky had foretold had arrived. I could hear the patter of the raindrops as they beat against the boarded windows, while the wind whistled dismally outside.

A night alone with the dead! I don't think it was intention on her part, but the chair was back to the door by which we had entered the room, and placed at just such an angle that when I looked straight ahead, the grim, stark body of my victim was directly in my line of vision. The storm raging outside suggested my similarity to a ship in a storm at sea, battling with over-powering elements against which it was arrayed. That was it; I was a storm tossed ship upon the bosom of the Sea of Life, and my adversaries were the tempest that was slowly bringing about my destruction.

Already our commercial business was feeling the effects of Fitzgerald's power, as only this afternoon we had received word from two of our oldest customers, who had kept a standing order with us for years, that beginning with the next month their business would be transferred to an opposing concern. And I knew this to be only the beginning.

The storm was gaining in violence, while the rain still beat against the window-boards, but it came in torrents now. I strained at my bonds with a sudden fury, and struggled desperately until the cords cut deep ridges into my wrists and ankles. At last I realized the futility of endeavoring, and gave up in hopeless despair. The slam of the outside door brought me bolt upright in my chair. Had the girl come back for something or other she had forgotten, or was this some new factor in the situation, some new danger that beset me? The click of heels upon the bare floor was distinctly feminine, but the footsteps bore little resemblance to those of the Italian girl. "Chester! Chester Brent!"

I must be dreaming! Could I believe my ears? If only it was really true!

"Here! This way!" I called into the darkness. "Can you find me?"

"Coming," sang out the voice, cheerily.

My optimism rose several degrees. My old-time confidence was returning by leaps and bounds. I heard the swish of skirts behind my chair, and in another moment Anita Burgess stood before me.

"The right pocket of my inside coat. My knife."

She understood. A few quick slashes, and I was free.

"I saw you when you came in with the girl," she told me, "and I saw the man when he arrived. I thought I heard a pistol shot, and feared for you safety. When the girl came out alone I knew that something out of the ordinary had happened, for they always came out together. I let her get safely out of the way before I dared to leave my hiding-place in the shadows across the way. A skeleton key did the rest, and here I am. The man? Where has he gone?"

"Dead!" I indicated the body at the other end of the room. "I had to do it in self-defense. I didn't intend to kill him."

She shrugged her shoulders.

"Perhaps it is just as well. At least he is one stumbling-block removed from our path."

"But how did you know I was coming here?"

"I didn't; that part of it was a surprise. It was the man I was lying in wait for, for I knew he had stolen my dragon ring. I knew that he met the girl here every night between eleven and twelve, for I had followed him here before. Tonight I anticipated him."

"I have the ring." I took it from my pocket and gave it to her. "But the documents, the girl took them with her."

Miss Burgess wrinkled her brows thoughtfully.

"I think I know where she is bound. There is an even chance that we may be able to overtake her. My machine is waiting just a ways down the road. Are you still armed?"

"No; the girl took my revolver, too."

"I have an extra one in the automobile. Luckily I tossed it in at the last moment, as I feared losing the one I usually carry. Come, let us be off."

There was little need of further caution, so far at this house was concerned, so we wended our way through the maze of empty rooms until at last we stepped out into the night.

The tempest had reached the zenith of its fury, causing jagged flashes of lightening to leap across the sky, relieving, momentarily, the stygian blackness of the heavens. The thunder crashed and rolled in mighty awe-inspiring detonations, like the roar of guns upon battlefields. A thunderstorm of such severity at this season of the year, when the autumnal winds were already making themselves felt and top-coats were appearing with increasing frequency, was extraordinary. In all probability it was the last storm of the season, and the elements seemed allied to give us one that we would be sure to remember.

How it did rain! Blinding sheets of it that bewildered, that one must battle against every step of the way. In spite of my protecting ulster I was soaked to the skin before we reached the runabout that waited only a short block away. I doubt if Miss Burgess, her long raincoat buttoned up under her chin, fared as ill at the hands of the storm as I. No chauffeur was waiting in the little machine at the corner, and Miss Burgess waved me into my seat, started the motor at the first turn of the crank, climbed into her place behind the wheel, put on the gear, and we plunged into the storm.

I fell to marveling at the versatility of the girl beside me. Fearless, cool and collected in an emergency; capable of handling a situation that would deviate stouter hearts from their tasks; her familiarity with firearms; and now the masterful way in which she drove the car over the slippery pavements; one would not look for such a variety of accomplishments in her type. I speculated in what way she might next show her superiority over the majority of the vapid, namby-pamby, doll-like creatures I knew, who set themselves up as typical of American womanhood.

CHAPTER TEN

A BEAST AT BAY

MISS BURGESS applied the brakes with a suddenness that nearly threw me out of my seat; the machine skidded several yards over the wet asphalt under its own momentum before she finally brought it to a standstill.

"There she is now."

My eyes penetrated the gloom until I, too, caught sight of the rain-soaked figure just ahead. She was plodding on through the storm, unheeding the wind that whistled about her ears or the rain that poured down in never ending torrents. Her wet, boyish clothes clung to her well-rounded figure.

We followed along in the machine, keeping at a respectful distance, and I took this opportunity to narrate my experiences in detail to Miss Burgess from the time we had parted at the house in the country until she had rescued me. I told of the attempted robbery at my apartments, my interview with Fitzgerald, and the events of the early evening.

"In spite of all our precautions the package got away from me."

"Don't worry," she assured, "we still have a chance to regain it. If my suppositions are correct, we are still due for experiences before the sun rises again."

The storm was abating, and the torrential downpour had given place to a disagreeable drizzle.

Now that I was myself once more, I yearned for action. This sitting back in an automobile, trailing along at a snail's pace after a girl who had bested me twice in a single night, was galling. Had I had my way, I would have pounced upon that lone figure from behind and wrested the documents away from her by sheer brute force.

Steadily the boyish figure of the Italian girl kept on. We had gained an aristocratic quarter of the city, and at last our quarry mounted the steps on an impressive dwelling. We watched until a light gleamed in the hall, and the door opened to admit the girl. Another light flashed from behind shades where darkness had been before, and we knew then in what part of the house the next act of our little drama was to be staged. The light shone from the window of an upstairs apartment, leaving the downstairs in darkness, except for the front hallway. This setting was admirably suited to our present plans. If the interview had taken place downstairs our chances of discovery in trying to force an entrance would have been trebled. Miss Burgess drove to the end of the block, rounded the corner, and we left the machine just as the storm ceased. The clouds had vanished, and tiny stars were peeping at us from a clear sky.

I wondered if this circumstance was prophetic of our situation, if the events ahead were to clear up the mystery that surrounded us and leave everything as calm and peaceful as before.

Our next task was to find a way to enter the house without being apprehended. First we tried the windows. We had almost completely circled the house before I found one that slid up under the pressure I brought to bear. Cautiously, carefully, I drew myself up and through. Then I gave Miss Burgess a hand. With the agility of a boy she clambered to a place at my side, and we silently closed the window. The extra six-shooter Miss Burgess had so thoughtfully provided nestled close at hand in my coat pocket. I could see the glint of her own weapon as she prepared to locate the stairway leading to the upper floor.

We had the light in the hall to guide our search, so it was only a matter of seconds before we located the stairs. Fearful lest some slight sound might arouse servants, we exercised the utmost care in ascending the stairs. As we reached the top, the hum of voices fell upon our ears, and a lighted room indicated our goal. We doubled our vigilance, and crept along close to the wall until we brought up just outside the half-opened door from which we distinctly heard the girl we trailed saying:

"But I tell you I will have nothing more to do with this affair."

All the color, all the snap and vitality had gone from her voice. She spoke in a dull, droning monotone.

"Miss Sabastino, at the present time I positively cannot allow you to do as you suggest. You are in possession of too much information. I must insist that you stick by your original agreement. Any deviation would be extremely unwise."

The sound of the man's voice was a decided surprise. I had not the least suspicion until then that the "boss" who directed her movements was R. F. Fitzgerald. The fact that my room had been raided while he and I were dining together had rather thrown me off the track. I had imagined that perhaps there were two factions struggling for the possession of that mysterious package. Then he must have known all the while we were together that my rooms were being searched. This new turn of affairs added to my bewilderment. What did that package contain that he had gone to such extremes to get it into his hands?

The time was now ripe for action.

Miss Burgess placed her lips close to my ear, and whispered: "You cover the girl; I'll take care of the man myself."

The two were so engrossed in their conversation that they were all unconscious of our presence in the room until Miss Burgess commanded:

"Just raise your hands well above your heads, my friends." Obediently two pair of arms shot into the air, and at the sight of me the Italian girl acted as if she had seen a ghost.

"Good evening," I bantered. "You see, I did not have to wait until morning for your assistance, Miss Sabastino."

She cringed. One could see that her iron will was broken, her dominant spirit gone. Her lips quivered, and she struggled to keep back the tears that even now glistened in her eyes. When she spoke her voice faltered, wavered, almost broken.

"You can count on no more trouble from me, Mr. Brent. I have just informed Mr. Fitzgerald that I was about to sever my connections with this affair. Rollo"—she bit her lip in a supreme effort to control herself as she mentioned the dead man's name "Rollo was mean to me, at times even cruel—but—but—I loved him! And now he is dead!"

Oblivious of the threat of my leveled revolver, she dropped into a chair and buried her head in her arms, her shoulders shaking with silent sobs. The rain-water trickling in little rivulets from her saturated garments, the heaving of her bosom as she sobbed her heart out in grief for the man she loved, combined to make her a pitiful picture of abject despair. The effect of her collapse on the other occupants of the room was varied in the extreme.

For my own part my conscience twinged with sudden qualms, for I was the instrument by which her sweetheart had come to his sudden end. Fitzgerald's thick, sensuous lips curled into an ugly sneer, expressive of his disgust for the girl's weakness in yielding thus to her emotions, and Miss Burgess darted one quick, sympathetic glance in her direction, then her features resumed their mask of immobility.

"That rather simplifies matters, Mr. Brent. Suppose you go through this man's pockets, while I keep him covered with this toy. If will be perfectly safe. He knows I wouldn't hesitate in the least to shoot him if he made an unnecessary move."

I emptied Fitzgerald's pockets swiftly, and efficiently, and found that he was unarmed. I piled the contents of his pockets on the table.

"Now, Mr. Brent, if you will take care of him while I look over these trinkets," suggested Miss Burgess. "Mr. Fitzgerald may be seated if he desires, as long as he doesn't attempt to lower those hands."

I could hear the click of his teeth as he snapped his jaws together in a rage. Again I was reminded of the cat—or was it the leopard—in his manner, only this time the semblance was that of a cat-beast at bay. He chanced a step forward, but the determination in my eyes, coupled with the unwavering weapon in my hand, checked him. He took Miss Burgess' suggestion and made himself as comfortable as possible in a handy easy-chair. If it had not been such a serious matter, the sight of this potbellied, prosperous-looking business man, with his hands thrust grotesquely above his head, would have been funny.

Miss Burgess sorted the articles of which I had deprived him, and selected a letter or two, which went into her hand-bag. I caught her humming snatches of a popular air as she began a systematic search of the room. The place was evidently Fitzgerald's sanctuary. At nearly every turn she found something which went into her spacious bag. She uttered a happy little cry as she discovered a small, red, morocco-bound book, and scanned its contents before depositing it in her bag with the rest of her finds. Fitzgerald had half-turned in his chair at her enthusiastic cry, and at the sight of the book she had unearthed, he swore volubly. I feared for a moment he contemplated launching his huge bulk at the girl, but he thought better of it, and settled back into his chair.

Miss Burgess was still humming when she had completed the search, and her bag bulged with the weight of its contents. There was a phone at the end of the room, and to this she next turned her attention.

"Is this the Department of Justice? This is Douglass' operative No. 2291, Anita Burgess. You'd better send some men up to Fitzgerald's—yes, R. F. Fitzgerald's—I've got enough evidence to convict him a hundred times. There's a girl here, too, who, I think, will be invaluable to us as a witness. Yes, I'll wait for them, but send them right along. My prisoner isn't any too docile, and there's many a slip, you know. All right; good-bye."

The receiver clicked into position.

"Douglass' operative No. 2291!" That could mean nothing except the Douglass Detective Agency that had recently been proving of great assistance to the government in hunting out undesirable alien enemies.

"There, that's over. I fear, Mr. Fitzgerald, that you will sleep in a strange bed tonight, but you'll have ample opportunity to get familiar with it. All we can do now, Mr. Brent, is wait for the men the department is sending."

The package the girl had taken from me was lying, still unopened, on the center table, and my glance rested on it for a moment.

"The documents," I reminded her; "what about those?"

"Oh, those?" Her rippling laughter rang musically upon my ears. "You may open it now, if you like, Mr. Brent. I'll take charge of my prisoner while you do so. It's quite likely he is still interested in the contents, too."

At last I was to learn the secret of the package. It took me what seemed an eternity to break the seal. My fingers were all thumbs. Eventually I held the contents in my hands, and spread the pages out, expectantly.

Imagine my chagrin, my mortification, as I realized that the documents I had so carefully guarded, the important papers that Fitzgerald had been so anxious to obtain, were nothing more nor less than several sheets of folded, blank paper!

CHAPTER ELEVEN

THE WHOLE TRUTH

FITZGERALD'S FACE grew purple with rage at the revelation, while I was nonplussed for a brief moment. Then, I, too was filled with a sense of outraged dignity. To think that I had been hoodwinked into safeguarding a package that contained nothing but blank paper! I was bewildered, confounded, disheartened, humiliated and abashed in quick succession.

Miss Burgess was quick to notice my changing expression.

"Don't feel badly over it, Mr. Brent, or feel that you've been made a fool of. The package served its purpose—to aid in bringing this treacherous snake to justice. I know it is all a puzzle to you, that with the facts at your disposal you cannot quite fathom it. But it's a long story. The men from the department are due at any moment. It's nearly morning, and I'm pretty well used up after the nervous strain I've been under the last few weeks. Suppose we leave the telling for some future time. If I may suggest it, we might dine together tomorrow night at a quiet place I know; then, I promise, I shall tell you the whole interesting truth of the affair."

Her reasoning was sound. I could ask no fairer arrangement. She told me where she wished to dine; we set the time, and the bargain was sealed.

The police came just then, and an astounded butler, awakened by their vigorous ringing, let them in. A still more astounded butler, wide awake now, watched them handcuff his master to them ignominiously. The girl promised to go along without this indignity, and Miss Burgess vouched for her safety. I realized that my Lady of the Dragon was a keen analyst of character, for my knowledge of her abilities was growing. In spite of the lateness of the hour, Miss Burgess insisted on driving me to my apartments, where she left me with a parting injunction to remember our dinner appointment for the next evening.

Just as if there were any danger of my forgetting! I looked forward to that explanation with the eagerness a small boy looks forward to a fishing trip with dad. The restaurant she had selected was quiet and unobtrusive, ideally adapted for a meeting of this kind.

I reached the place far in advance of the time set for our appointment, and fretted and fumed at my idiocy in being so infernally early as I paced to and fro in front of the place, awaiting her arrival. My wait would have been needless had I been on time, for Miss Burgess was punctual to the minute.

"Mr. Brent," she began, when we were at last comfortably settled at one of the tables, "first I must apologize for several necessary falsehoods I told you, and for the deception in regard to the contents of the package which caused you so much trouble. Fact and fiction are so intermingled in the garbled version you have of the affair, I had better start at the very beginning, and this is all how it came about:

"My father died just after the war broke out. He had met with serious financial reverses just previous to his death, and left my mother and I practically penniless. I shall always feel that worrying over the impending crash hastened his death. After the estate was settled, I knew, if we used the slightest remainder to live upon, it would soon be eaten up, and mother and I would be, figuratively speaking, thrown upon the world. I realized that I must find some sort of work at which I could support the two of us. Opportunity beckoned through an influential friend, and I accepted a position with the Douglass Detective Agency. Once well into the work, I reveled in it. I put my whole heart and soul into every task assigned to me, and gradually I came to be used for more hazardous work. Blind luck, more than anything else, aided me in bringing my first few bigger cases to a successful conclusion.

"A short time ago I received instructions to work under the direction of the Department of Justice for the duration of the war. Fitzgerald had been under the surveillance of the department for several months. They suspected his connection with the Central Powers, but needed some positive proof before they dared make an arrest. He was wary. In spite of all their attempts to force his hand, he bided his time. Whatever moves he made were executed in absolute secrecy. Uncle Sam never gives up. Once the government of the United States sets itself against you, you might as well throw up your hands. The men were unable to procure anything in the way of tangible evidence. Very well, if the men failed, put a woman on the job! I was the woman.

"At the earliest possible moment an introduction between Fitzgerald and me was arranged. I proceeded to cultivate his acquaintance. At the same time rumors were started destined to reach the ears of Fitzgerald. These rumors had it that I was in possession of a formula, made by my father, for an explosive more powerful, more deadly than TNT— which, as you know, is the most powerful explosive the world has ever known. If Fitzgerald was, as we suspected him, in the pay of the German government, he would be desirous of obtaining this formula before the allies had a chance to open negotiations for it.

"In the hours I spent in the company of this man, I purposely avoided all reference to the subject, but the rumors fostered by the department persisted. Finally he began to be interested. Of course, he was too wise to allow me to know that he was interested. My first clue to his interest was when I came home one evening, after a theater party and midnight supper—with Fitzgerald—to surprise some one in the act of searching my room.

"Douglass put him through the third degree, but he might just as well have tried getting blood out of a stone. The ruffian denied all knowledge of any such person as R. F. Fitzgerald, or any other party by that name. No way had yet been devised for forcing a man to tell the truth. The only excuse we had for holding him was on a charge of attempted burglary. Acting upon a suggestion from Douglass, the judge gave the culprit a limit sentence.

"In order that Fitzgerald might not suspect I connected him with the episode, I doubled my attentions towards him. It was then that Bassino came into the affair. He was an adventurer, pure and simple. Although Italian, his love of money was greater than his love of country. You should have been at the department this morning when the girl told how she had been forced to serve his ends against her will. Like many another good woman she had thrown herself away on a worthless scoundrel; and despite the many heartaches and troubles he caused her, she loved him deeply, fiercely. She holds Fitzgerald responsible for her lover's untimely end, and swears vengeance by all the saints. Her willingness to tell what she knows will most likely let her off with a light sentence. But I am straying from the main line.

"Bassino's espionage was worthy of a more deserving cause. Inside a week he had established my connection with the department, and Fitzgerald dropped me as he would a hot coal. I was confronted with the possibility of failure. So far I had proven a match for every task to which I had been assigned, and was resolved that I would not fall down on this problem. I would work out the solution in my own way.

"I cast about for some new method of attack, and analyzed the business of the man, after which I made a list of the people with whom his business brought him into direct contact. In doing so, of course, I included your name. My father had told me the story of the dragon rings, and the oath of fealty connected with them, and had given his ring to me with a request that I respect the vows he had made.

"'Brent' is not a common name, and the fact that it was the same as the owner of the other ring, commanded my attention. If you were only a descendent of my father's old chum, perhaps I could use the ring to enlist your assistance; that is, if you knew the story of the ring and held sacred the oath your father had taken. It was worth a chance. So I investigated your family history. I went to Manorport, as I told you. I did not do it secretly, however. Far from it. I knew that Bassino, or some one else, was in full knowledge of my every move. That was as I wished. If you became involved in the affair,

Fitzgerald would know of it within half an hour. Then I must stake all on the chance of your connection with the matter forcing him to make some unguarded move.

"When I found out you were actually the son of Peter Brent I began my campaign. The element of mystery which surrounded my anonymous note and the queer card was to stimulate your interest in the affair. I must have some plausible excuse for asking you to help me, so I fixed up the packet of 'documents' and connected the story I told you. I relied upon your knowledge of the ring and your natural impulsiveness to make you willing to 'go it blind.' You see, I had picked up a great deal of information about you in Manorport that proved of great assistance in formulating my plans. The result of our interview exceeded my wildest expectations.

"I don't know where the 'leak' was in your office, but I do know that Fitzgerald was in possession of every detail of that interview within the hour. I could not have asked for more. You can readily see the importance of keeping that package away from him. Had he discovered that it contained only blank paper, my ruse would have been exposed, my last chance of outwitting him, gone. My other requests for secrecy were simply to impress you more thoroughly, to make you realize the importance of the affair without giving you any real information.

"Practically all the rest of the events you know. That morocco-bound book was a code-book that will help in deciphering several important papers which have fallen into our hands. The other things I took away with me were letters and documents that not only absolutely convict Fitzgerald of being a spy in the pay of the German government, but also implicate parties of national reputation whom we never would have in the least suspected."

So that was the answer to the riddle. It was all simple enough now that the facts were laid before me.

"I trust, Mr. Brent," she was saying, "that just because your connection with this matter is at an end, it will not mean a severance of our relations."

I thrilled at the possibilities contained in the thought. "Your sentiments coincide with mine, Miss Burgess, to the letter."

I helped her into her wrap and we made our way leisurely to the street, where I hailed a taxi.

"Now that the ban of secrecy is lifted, may I have the privilege of seeing you home—Anita?"

Her blue eyes looked full into mine, searchingly, intently. Her eyelids drooped over them, and she turned partly away as she responded:

"I think you may—Chester."

As we bowled along over the cobblestones my mind was a seething caldron of conflicting emotions. Hope and fear, joy and gloom, happiness and despair, played tag with one another around my tired brain.

In an overwhelming flash it came to me. I knew that this girl at my side was the one girl of all girls in the world for me. Fate had crossed threads of our destinies, and I knew that as surely as there were stars in the heavens that some day I would make her my very own, my Lady of the Dragon.

www.ingramcontent.com/pod-product-compliance
Lightning Source LLC
Chambersburg PA
CBHW050911120626
46552CB00004B/1508